First published in 2015.
This paperback published 2015.

First Edition ISBN: 978-1-911076-21-6
Second Edition ISBN: 978-1-911076-23-0

Pamela Harry

IT'S A LONG LIFE

SECOND EDITION

Thank you to all my dachshund loving friends,
who encouraged me to publish these words.

THE FOX CUB

My name is Enzo
And my sister's name is Fleur
And we were sitting quietly when
Something outside caused a stir

Mum thought at first was a kitten
About nine on Saturday night
But then saw that it was a fox cub
Setting off our security light

Well this cheeky cub in our garden
Started peering through our kitchen door
And Fleur let out a couple of barks
But I really gave it what for

Our mum would not let us out though
Which we thought was really unfair
But she had to once it was bedtime
And we searched then everywhere

But despite our super keen noses
The fox cub was not to be found
So must have been very well hidden
And didn't make one single sound

And so to bed in the kitchen
While mum went upstairs to join dad
But as soon as she'd got herself settled
She knew we would drive her mad

The fox cub had come out of hiding
So again we created mayhem
It had even been joined by it's mother
So of course we were barking at them

Mum tried very hard to calm us
And a second time went up to bed
But in the end she stayed down with us
As we had other ideas instead

And so we went into the lounge
And hoped then to get some rest
But still we could hear the foxes call
And only got snatches at best

At 3.00 o'clock in the morning
Our dad came down for a moan
The noise was keeping him from his sleep
And yet he'd slept hours on his own

And later on that morning
We went with our mum outside
And Fleur kept sniffing at one certain spot
Where mum thought the fox cub could hide

Well 9.00 o'clock on Sunday night
There was barking and screaming again
Mummy fox was coaxing her cub
But her efforts were all in vain

But enough was enough by midnight
And so we were carried upstairs
Another night with so little sleep
Would've been a poor state of affairs

And so to keep us both settled
Between mum and dad was our place
But then they were falling out of their bed
As we left them so little space

At 6.00 a.m. mum brought us down
After a somewhat restless night
And again we rushed round the garden
But there wasn't a fox now in sight

Still we could hear them calling
Mummy fox was in such distress
But the back wall to their 'home' garden
Was too tall for the fox cub I guess

THE FOX CUB

Mum saw the cub in the garden next door
So maybe a new way was found
But after a better Monday night
The fox cub was still around

It had stayed in next door's garden
But was crying now all on it's own
I think mummy fox has given up
And abandoned her cub all alone.

THE FOX CUB SEQUEL

And so we have the sequel
To the little fox cub's plight
But only after it had spent
Another lonely night

Our neighbour couldn't catch it
And still we heard it cry
As it was just too clever
Or maybe you'd say sly

She rang the local services
Who didn't want to know
But then she rang a Fox Catcher
Relocator to have a go

And in the early afternoon
The fox cub then was caught
They found she was a vixen
In good health although distraught

They took her five doors down
To the home from which she'd come
Where once again she joined
Her three siblings and her mum

And now the noise has stopped
The quiet seems so strange
And sleep did not come easy
As the peace made such a change

And so our mum won't worry
When it's time to let us out
Though left to Fleur and me
There'd be a different end no doubt.

NAUGHTY DARCEY

Time to go out
So mum opened the door
And the wind blasted rain
All over the floor

She knew at once
That we would protest
She had seen 'the look'
But it was no contest

It was time for bed
So there wasn't a choice
And meanie mummy
Denied us a voice

So out we went
As she wasn't joking
And all of us then
Got a thorough soaking

But where was Darcey?
She wasn't outside
And so our mum hunted
As she was trying to hide

And then it was spotted
A Darcey puddle
So the naughty culprit
Jumped up for a cuddle

But was she naughty
Or would you say wise
When getting a cuddle
With her cute puppy eyes?

While we were all wet
So no cuddles for us
But we got a towel dry
A warm bed and some fuss.

INVASION TWO

We have a new invader
A plumber man has come
Because we had a little flood
Which didn't please our mum

She'd been with friends for coffee
When a pipe began to leak
And water spurted for three hours
Which flooded the en-suite

Also the utility room
Had water on the floor
So water off and mopping up
Was our poor mum's next chore

It seemed to take forever
Which meant our tea was late
But mum was just not happy
So we simply had to wait

Dad hadn't even noticed
And so the water spread
Creeping under skirting boards
Which made our mum see red

Thankfully the floors are tiled
And finally all was dry
Then mum sat down exhausted
But we thought that she might cry

And so we softly nuzzled her
In usual dachsie style
As all of us know very well
Just how to make mum smile

So then we got our dinner
And mummy got hers too
And two days on the plumber came
To put all back to new

He took the boxing off the pipes
And changed the damaged section
And when he turned the water on
It passed the leak inspection

It cost a lot of money
But mum was just relieved
And now she's fixed the dishwasher
So something else achieved.

THE ROBBERS

Today's the day the rubbish men
Come to steal our waste
So we make sure that we all bark
So they retreat in haste

It maybe only rubbish
But it belongs to us
So it is only right that we
Should make the biggest fuss

We don't think they're afraid though
As it's all done with tail wags
While hoping they enjoy the whiff
From two weeks of dog bags

Our Gemma's at the forefront
She likes to think she's tough
But she could find much better use
For all this doggie stuff

We're sure it really has to pong
Out in the sunshine
But it is all part of their job
Which we think is divine

It's good if they remember us
We think we make them smile
Which gets them through their busy day
Whilst taking our dog pile

Our boxes are now empty
And our wheelie bin is back
But we'll be here and waiting
When next they rob our pack.

DIGGING DARCEY

My name is Darcey
And I've been in mummy's pots
But I'm hoping that she forgives me
Because she loves me lots

I've also been in the flowerbeds
And made a bit of a mess
It's just that I so love digging
But I don't mean to cause her stress

And now the pots are empty
So I think that mum's given up
And put the plants in the compost
As she thinks I'm a naughty pup

She has replanted twice already
So has probably had enough
It was super fun while it lasted
But dachshund life can be tough

And now the gate to the garden
Is closed all because of me
And so my brothers and sisters
Have sent me to Coventry

I really hope mum soon relents
And opens the gate once more
My pack mates don't like the restriction
And I also think that it's a bore

I'll try very hard to be good
If the temptation isn't too great
And no doubt my mum will be watching
So my digging will just have to wait.

REGAL KIRSTY

I'm the regal Kirsty
And my mum's at my beck and call
I gave her three gorgeous daughters
So she doesn't mind at all

The others get up in the morning
When they know it's time to be fed
But I sleep on and wait patiently
Till I'm brought my breakfast in bed

And when I've finished eating
I'm delivered a warmed bowl of milk
But I do feel these cotton covers
Ought to be made of silk

And so with my bowls now empty
I'm carried to our garden loo
And then of course I go back to bed
As more beauty sleep now is due

I never eat with the rabble
So when it's time for our tea
Mine is brought to the sitting room
And I have it on the settee

And when mum sits down for a coffee
And hopes for a chance to relax
I nudge at her arm for attention
As her priority should be this dax

I think it makes her fed up though
As sometimes her coffee gets spilled
But her protests won't ever stop me
As I am very strong willed

And last thing at night before bedtime
I give dad the run around
And jump at my mum for a carry
As it's her job to take out this hound

And then my place is a pillow
Right above my mum's head
But I'm happy to share my space with her
As I know that it's really her bed

Life's great as a regal dachshund
I deserve all that I can get
Some would say that I'm spoilt
But I know I'm just mum's pampered pet.

BARKING

We'll bark if you move too quickly
We'll bark if you leave your chair
We'll bark if we hear a noise outside
In case there's a stranger there

We'll bark if another dog barks
We'll bark if someone's in our road
We'll bark if a bird flies close to the ground
But the doorbell just makes us explode

We'll howl if you dare to leave us
As we think you'll never come back
And once we get going we're deafening
So you really should not leave this pack

Tessa will bark if she hears a fly
And she barks at the hoover as well
Kirsty just likes the sound of her voice
But Gemma's the barker from hell

Amber barks at the hosepipe
And gets herself wet through and through
And Lewis and Sophie will both bark for treats
As they always know when they are due

Bailey will bark at our mealtimes
Whilst spinning around and around
And Pippa gives out a high pitched squeak
But Darcey's the quieter hound

And even with no barking reason
We'll bark just to know that we can
But our mum keeps trying to stop us
So we think that she's no barking fan

There are others with multiple dachshunds
Who know the addiction is bad
But our mum quite simply can't help herself
And some say she's barking mad

We so hope that after our house move
We'll have neighbours just too far away
To be bothered about all our barking
So we can bark unrestricted each day.

THE HEATWAVE

Our mum has bought a sprinkler thing
And stuck it on the hose
We'd not seen one of these before
So thought we'd have a nose

It didn't look exciting
And it didn't smell at all
But when mum turned the tap on
It became a waterfall

We didn't know which way to run
It sprayed from side to side
With water shooting everywhere
There was no place to hide

We thought it was a dirty trick
To catch us by surprise
You'd think that she would pick on
Someone closer to her size

And now she's filled a paddling pool
We're worried what's in mind
She knows we don't like water
So she can't be that unkind

But sure enough our Amber
Was the first one to be caught
And plonked right in the middle
Our mum's such a rotten sport

And so we knew we'd not escape
But then we found it cool
To chill in this hot heatwave
In our brand new paddling pool

We thought it only fair though
That our mum should get wet too
And splashed the water everywhere
Until she was wet through.

TOO HOT

It's too hot to be a hot dog
It's too hot in this heatwave
It's too hot to wear a long fur coat
But we longs must not have a shave

It's too hot to sleep in the night
And it's too hot under the cover
It's too hot even to snuggle our mum
But she knows either way that we love her

It's so great to see the sunshine
But this humidity is far too much
And even all of our paving slabs
Are just too hot to the touch

So it's too hot to go for a walk
Except if it's early or late
And still it can be too hot
So we'd rather stay home now and wait

It's also too hot for our mum
Although she has so little fur
She struggles now with her workload
So we try to be good just for her

But it's even too hot for our plants
So although it's too hot to move
Mum knows she must give them a drink
Until weather conditions improve

It's Not to hot for the midges though
And they all seem to go after mum
So these long coats can be quite useful
As to us they never do come

And it's not too hot for the flies
That keep buzzing all through our house
They seem to drive Tessa crazy
She's just like a cat with a mouse

She's so quick that sometimes she'll catch them
And of course she just has to bark
So then the rest of us must join in
It's a good job they sleep when it's dark

Tommorrow they say will be cooler
We think our mum's hoping for rain
She says that our garden needs it
Then we'll be wishing for sunshine again.

DAYLIGHT

With daylight hours so long now
Most of us wake up at six
But yesterday and the day before
At five mum was woken with licks

She really was most unimpressed
But still had to let us outside
And then she went straight back to bed
As this early she could not abide

She'd been woken all through the night
Four times she had been disturbed
So to then have to get up at five
Was to her completely absurd

It's always the same usual dogs
And Gemma's a guarantee
Pippa's unwell and can't help herself
But it's also the boys and Sophie

The chocolates are never a bother
And always sleep right through the night
They'd happily sleep until 9.00 o'clock
It's no matter that it is daylight

But today we waited till six
So mum thinks the message got through
That breakfast was not to be had
Until she considered it due.

WASPS

Mum loves the summer but hates the flies
The ones that buzz or bite
But she really hates the stinging wasps
She can't even bear the sight

They are so very nasty
And seem to sting for fun
And even when they've got you
It doesn't mean they're done

Three times a wasp had stung her
Though she made it pay the price
But she worries for her dachshunds
As she knows it isn't nice

Our Molly once was stung
And mum rushed her to the vet
She very nearly died that day
So she never will forget

She worries most for Tessa
Who chases all on wings
She thinks she's our protector
From all these flying things

Thankfully she barks so much
That mum is made aware
And promptly then removes the threat
That gives her such a scare

Darcey's such a nosey pup
And still so very young
She's always into everything
So mum hopes she's not stung

But often in the autumn time
When stingers are around
Our noses are most vulnerable
As they're crawling on the ground

Mum does her best to keep us safe
And sometimes has to scold
But she knows we dachshunds aren't the best
For doing as we're told

So she simply has to live in hope
And do all that she can
To get through stinging season
While these wasps end their lifespan.

TREATS

Mum has placed an order
And our treats are on the way
So we're waiting for the courier man
Who we think will come today

And sure enough a van pulls up
Right outside our gate
Mum knows the seller well
So they never do come late

We then jump up at our front door
And make our usual din
While mum sneaks out the kitchen way
To get our treats box in

She puts it on the worktop
Whilst we sit with longing eyes
And opens up our package
To reveal our favourite prize

It isn't really treats time
But we know mum won't ignore
The pleading looks we give her
As she's seen it all before

You cannot beat the dachshund gaze
So even when we've had one
A second treat would go down well
Unless mum says we're done

Sometimes she feels generous
But sometimes she's just tight
So one is all that we can get
Until the time is right.

BONES

Our dad's been to the butcher shop
And asked the nice man there
If for nine hungry dachshunds
He had bones that he could spare

Well he disappeared a moment
And then handed dad a bag
Full of yummy meaty bones
For a guaranteed tail wag

And when our dad came home
The smell near drove us mad
Fresh bones are our most favourite thing
That we have ever had

Mum took the bag outside
And we could scarcely wait
As each of us was given one
This butcher's our top mate

We chewed on them for hours
And didn't want our tea
So that was one cheap meal
When these bones had all been free

And now we are exhausted
But we know our mum will keep
All our bony leftovers
While we catch up on sleep

These bones will keep us gnawing
For several more days yet
Until dad asks our butcher mate
If more bones he can get.

ROLLING GEMMA

At 7.00 o'clock this evening
Our Amber thought she'd go
And when mum caught me rolling
I was covered head to toe

Well straight away she hosed me down
Which wasn't very kind
But after she had dried me off
I really didn't mind

But now I'm playing shadow
And giving puppy looks
As all that I'm now wanting
Is to be in mum's good books

I know my little episode
That got both of us plastered
Now needs the typical technique
That all dachshunds have mastered

The big sad eyes that never fail
She tries hard to be cross
But knows that she'll give in
Even though she is the boss

She doesn't understand
That I have this certain craving
As to me it's only natural
And not me misbehaving

But now I smell of vanilla
And sandalwood from a spray
My fragrance was much nicer before
Is all I have to say

I think mum thinks that I'll have learnt
And that I'll now refrain
From doing all my rolling
(Till I get my chance again).

GROOMING

With our eyes and ears cleaned
Mum trims 36 paws
And with teeth brushed and scraped
She grinds down 162 claws

Then we all are combed through
Removing any knots
As under our ears
Are our most common spots

Bath time in the shower
Is usually only tried
When the weather is warm
So we can dry off outside

But Gemma's the exception
Mum thinks she's a chore
With her dirty rolling habit
She needs showering more

She finds it a marathon
Which can feel quite a pain
As no sooner is it done
It needs doing again

But it makes it worthwhile
To see us all looking neat
As she so loves us groomed
With our trim tidy feet

Smooths would be easier
But she just likes the look
Of her long haired dachshunds
Who are tops in her book

And being a glutton for punishment
Her next long will come
When early next month
She becomes Elsie's mum.

THE CONVICTS

We have these horrid convict things
Trespassing at our place
And their black and yellow striped jackets
Are causing our mum's heart to race

First we had the hornets
With murder in their eyes
And now their nasty cell mates
So much smaller in their size

But still they can pack a punch
These wasps that sting just for fun
And one dared to enter our house last night
Which had our mum on the run

Three of us tried to catch it
As it crawled up our patio door
But then our mum started shouting at us
And knocked it down onto the floor

She picked it up with a tissue
Once she was sure it was dead
And told us they're not to be played with
And we should listen to what she has said

Darcey near nosed a hornet
While it was buzzing on the ground
But mummy was quick to tread on it
So lucky that she was around

Our Lewis then did the same
When he heard our mum screaming 'NO'
And another hornet met it's end
But will there be more to go?

Next to be yelled at was Darcey again
Mum saw her pick a wasp up
But promptly she dropped it without being stung
So a lucky escape for our pup

Mum can't wait for these horrid convicts
To meet their seasonal end
She cannot see what purpose they serve
As to her they are nobody's friend.

KIRSTY'S JOURNEY

Mum took us on a journey
So many miles from home
It was the longest day trip
That we have ever known

Just my daughter Darcey and I
Joined mummy for this ride
With a great big crate for the two of us
And a small one with no one inside

Eventually we stopped somewhere
And after tea and a chat
We both were put back in the car
And thought no more of that

Until the other lady
Handed our mum a pup
So the empty crate beside us
Would now be taken up

Mum had named her Elsie
And she cried much of the way
But for such a tiny puppy
It was just the longest day

This wasn't our only surprise though
As mum had another plan
We'd call on my other two daughters
Before our home trip began

Of course they're all grown up now
So maybe their memory had passed
But slowly the cogs were turning
And they remembered us at last

It made our mum so happy
And she'd have liked a longer stay
But we still had four hours of travel
So had to be on our way

And thirteen hours from leaving home
Our journey came to an end
And Elsie met her new family
With Darcey as her special friend

All of us were starving
And after we had been fed
Our exhausting day was over
And our only thought then was of bed.

INTRODUCING ELSIE

My name is Elsie
And I'm dachshund number 10
Mum knew that I would come one day
But just did not know when

I have now arrived though
So her once illusive cream
Has turned into reality
So no more need to dream

I'm loving life with my new friends
Especially with Darcey
I think she has adopted me
And wants to be my mummy

Other times we're playing
And she tries to beat me up
But I have pointy needle teeth
And am one feisty pup

Mum says that I'm a good girl
As I sleep right through the night
And mostly pees are done outside
One day I'll get it right

She found that I like cables
And was quick to spoil my fun
She thought it had gone quiet
When I had her laptop one

But I am just a puppy
And new things are so exciting
And while I have my baby teeth
There's so much here needs biting

Mum also found my gardening skills
Are not to be admired
As I do quite like digging
Which it seems is not desired

I'm only eight weeks old though
And I guess that I'll find out
The cans and can'ts of living here
And what life's all about.

THE MONSTER

Mum has this horrid monster thing
That makes this awful roar
She pushes it all round our house
And over every floor

There's nothing here that worries me
But this one's not much fun
It even has my brothers
And big sisters on the run

I saw it has a cable though
That follows everywhere
And so I thought I'd have a chew
Till mum gave me a scare

I heard her yelling NO
And then I heard her shout
If you attack my hoover
Then we two will both fall out

There are so many lessons
That it seems she has to teach
And now it's hung round door handles
To keep it from my reach

But I think I made it hard for her
And now she's given up
So the monster lost this battle
And I'm the winning pup.